THE ORIGIN OF MISS VICTORY

Evil Bore Not!

Stephen J. Cassinelli

Copyright © 2024 Stephen J. Cassinelli

eBook ISBN: 979-8-8692-6767-2
Paperback ISBN: 979-8-86926768-9
Hardcover ISBN: 979-8-8692-6778-8

All Rights Reserved. Any unauthorized reprint or use of this material is strictly prohibited. No part of this book may be reproduced or transmitted in any form or by any means, electronic or mechanical, including photocopying, recording, or by any information storage and retrieval system without express written permission from the author.

All reasonable attempts have been made to verify the accuracy of the information provided in this publication. Nevertheless, the author assumes no responsibility for any errors and/or omissions.

Table of Contents

DEDICATION — 1
Prologue — 3

Part 1
Chapter 1: Uncovering the Mysteries..........6
Chapter 2: A Gift from the Past..........13

Part 2
Chapter 3: The Hidden Castle's Secrets..........22
Chapter 4: The Perfect Specimen..........29
Chapter 5: Unveiling Shadows..........36

Part 3
Chapter 6: Vanishing Currents..........43
Chapter 7: The Birth of Miss Victory..........49
Chapter 8: Reflections and Reunion..........56

Acknowledgments: — 60
Coming Soon: — 61

DEDICATION

For those who have risked and given their lives, past, present, & future, so that others may live free.

Prologue

The Importance of Comic Books and Superheroes during World War II

Thank goodness for the patriotic-minded creators of comic book superheroes who remained keenly aware of global current affairs. They were the visionaries who foresaw the inevitable and responded by weaving tales within their publications—stories that served as warnings to readers, particularly children, long before America entered the impending war. The superheroes, who had recently burst onto the scene amidst the rise of Nazi Germany, unexpectedly found themselves assuming a new role far beyond mere entertainment. In fact, they became staunchly patriotic, embodying strong American values.

Comic books that battled the axis powers instilled in young readers a sense of the enemy long before they faced them on the battlefield. These stories, even within publications intended for a young audience, dared to expose the potential for evil. While much of it may have seemed fantastic, children are fortunately more receptive and adaptive to new concepts and ideas than adults. History has proven that these young adults, who later became soldiers, would rather die than be victims—enslaved and subjected to experiments like lab rats. These imaginative stories vividly depicted the horrors mankind is capable of, presenting astonishing ideas through colorful illustrations, showcasing the true nature of evil and what it takes to eradicate it.

By exposing the extraordinary and malevolent tactics employed by the forces of evil, these creations became an effective weapon against oppression, tyranny, and other forms of inhumane treatment towards fellow human beings. Superheroes and comic books seemingly emerged at the perfect time, as they warned against and combated malevolence, while also espousing patriotism and a love for country to their countless young readers. These very readers would later rise to the occasion, successfully defending the American way of life—cherishing freedom at all costs.

It is this author's opinion that comic books were one of the United States most powerful weapons against tyranny, why else would the government allow and actually encourage their production during a time when resources were scarce and the world was at war?

Part I

Chapter 1: Uncovering the Mysteries

EXTRA!!!! NEWS-FLASH!!!!!!! EXTRA!!!!

Read all about it! -

AMERICA'S FIRST PATRIOTIC SUPERHEROINE

At long last!

Origin discovered!

Who is she? Where did she come from?

As discovered and reported By Stephen Cascianelli, May 1, 2019

Fellow treasure hunters and friends of the superheroes, I have experienced the most amazing find of my life this past winter while searching for antiques and other treasures at a thrift store in Woonsocket, Rhode Island. Yes, I stumbled upon and purchased an early to mid-20th-century travel trunk, still in very good condition but stuck shut thanks to a rusted lock. The reason I purchased the trunk was that there appeared to be something inside. Using my father's famously fast-acting petroleum solvent lubricating oil, I soaked a rag and drenched the lock. After some wiggling and jiggling, and a few whacks with a hammer, I am happy to report that I managed to click the mechanism open without destroying the lock.

As soon as the trunk was opened, a musty odor spewed out—the smell of considerable age, mildew, and mothballs. Wrapped up in a white cotton blanket was what appeared to be an old piece of clothing.

Upon removal, I could see it was in a more old-school style, obviously hand-made, heavily worn women's red, white, and blue outfit—oddly modern, very high quality, and attractively designed. Whomever made it did a great job.

Upon closer examination, the outfit consisted of a long-sleeved flannel top that I first thought to be an old-time sports jersey. However, there were no buttons, numbers, or names stitched on it. Instead, a single white silk star was sewn on the front, dead center. When I lifted the top of the costume out of the trunk and shook the mothballs off, a heavy-duty blue and red cape attached to the back collar dropped down to just below the waist. This is when I assumed that what I found must be a costume of sorts. I was kinda bummed out, thinking this wasn't that great of a find. Obviously, it did get better from there.

Next to emerge was a pair of red leather or possibly vinyl shorts that felt much like an old Heart of the Hide leather baseball glove I used to play ball with. The leather was still quite soft, not dried up or brittle in the least. Attached to the shorts was a thick, heavy-duty, stainless steel-reinforced white leather belt with a large brass buckle. The front of the buckle was covered with shiny red plastic, possibly a Bakelite- type material.

There was also a pair of shiny red leather shoes—very streamlined, sleek, in the art deco style. They looked very futuristic, like something you would see in a sci-fi movie. Really cool-looking.

At the very bottom of the trunk, scattered about, there was a pair of thin red leather gloves tied to, I guess what you would call, a very low-profile double-sided black and white, super-minimalistic masquerade-type mask. Yes, at this time, I was convinced that what I found must have had something to do with a theatrical production or, hopefully, something used in a TV show or better yet, a movie.

As I started to put everything back, a group of folded papers fell out of an inside pocket. Printed in pen across the top middle fold in English, "This is my origin, Miss Victory." I unfolded the papers, and it was a handsomely handwritten letter, quite legible but in a language I couldn't understand, nor positively identify. It was signed on the last page. I set them aside.

My first instinct at this point was to Google Miss Victory, and I was quite surprised to see Miss Victory show up at the top of the first page because I never heard of her. I soon found out that Miss Victory was in fact a patriotic superheroine who appeared during the golden age of comic books, which I am aware began in the late 1930s prior to World War 2. Miss Vic's first exploit was published in the comic book Captain Fearless #1, published by Helnit Publications in August 1941.

When I scrolled down, there appeared a site known as Comic Book Plus that actually shows Miss Victory's very first episode in its entirety from Captain Fearless #1! I couldn't believe what I was looking at on the very first panel of the very first Miss Victory episode. The outfit Miss Victory was wearing and the outfit I had sitting before me appeared to be exactly the same. I assumed that what I found must be a replica, or perhaps a Halloween costume made by a fan of this long-forgotten woman superhero. I was a bit stumped and curious to learn more because I thought I knew or heard of all of the patriotic superheroes, especially females during that time, they were very limited. There was Wonder Woman and Lady Liberty and Miss America and I think there was also a Miss Patriot, but I had never heard of Miss Victory. What I realized at that moment was, I didn't know as much as I thought I did.

I had pretty much forgotten about the suit and was more interested in learning more about Miss Victory. Who was she? Where did she go? Who was she affiliated with? What team was she a part of?

I stayed up, skimming through the exploits that have been documented throughout the 2nd World War. Apparently, when the war came to an end, Miss Victory seemed to have fallen off the map, suddenly disappearing from the front lines of the patriotic superhero movement. Still, I could not find any information as to who Miss Victory was or where she came from. I had come to a dead end, and it was getting late, so I laid down, closed my eyes, and thought I might as well get some sleep. After about two or three minutes, my eyes opened up. The letter! It was already 3 a.m., and I was wired, there was no way I could sleep anyway. My second wind was kicking in and maybe a bit of adrenaline too.

While I was looking at the letter, I jumped on Google and started doing some comparative analysis, researching various languages. I found some similarities, but nothing that would be enough to establish any origin. So, I just started typing the letter as it is into my older computer's translation software, from unknown to English, and there it was! Bavarian. Without further ado, I proceeded to enter the entire letter into the translation app, then forwarded the English version to my email and printed it out.

Everything went as planned. Though a bit discombobulated, the translation was full of what appeared to be typographical errors. I have to admit, I was a bit dumbfounded. Was this fact or fiction? I was about to call it a night when I saw the sun was rising so I put on a fresh pot of coffee. I was on a mission.

As I was reading through the document, I came to realize, this wasn't something written for a production or a comic book, it was something else, much more personal, far more dramatic and a bit sad, almost like an entry into a diary, but too long to be that and it wasn't written in a book, just loose papers, as if the person who wrote it didn't stop until they were finished. I felt I was forcing myself to read it just as much as the author forced themselves to finish what they wanted to say. I had the sense that it was more of a statement, or possibly a testimonial or some sort of an affidavit but it wasn't notarized, though it was handwritten. My spidey senses were tingling fearing the worst until I got through it enough to realize that it wasn't a suicide letter, there's a happy ending. I think this is what they call a holographic type will?

I didn't find any of this information when I was researching earlier. I happened to glance up at the clock and to no surprise, it was already past nine, and my eyelids had been shutting down for the past half hour. The java buzz was gone and I needed to sleep so I put the transcript down and laid down on the couch. I didn't want to undress and get into bed, the mail-man would be around soon and if he had to knock on the door for a signature or had a package, I didn't want him to think I was still in bed past noon.

Without interruption I woke up abruptly, and felt as if I didn't sleep a wink but the clock said 4 o'clock so I must have really needed a rest. I had my clothes on so I checked the mailbox and the mailman certainly came by, there was a town paper and some other insignificant junk mail. I mixed up a glass of cold chocolate milk and made myself a tomato and cheese sandwich. About to lollygag about, I realized while there was still time, I better get on the phone and make a few calls.

Without further ado, I gave the Library of Congress a buzz, and after a solid 20-minute wait, plenty of time to eat my sandwich and check my email, a gentleman answered who identified himself as Martin Baker asking how he could help. Not quite sure where to begin, I started reading aloud from the notes I took earlier that morning. He listened patiently then stopped me when I got to the part about migrating to the United States in 1941 and suggested that I should get off the phone while there's still time and give the United States Immigration Bureau a call, extension 1941 and tell them exactly what I told him.

I went ahead and made the call and wouldn't you know it, the phone was answered before I heard it ring once! A young man, who was eating something, mumbled, "Records, can I help you". With little time to spare I started reading from my notes and when I got to the part about Miss Victory a superhero during WW2, the young man interrupted, "Contact the Comic Book Collectors Society, that's who you want to talk to. They have an office here in D.C." I heard a few tones and assumed he must have been transfering me but the phone went silent.. I looked at my watch and indeed, it was 5:01.

A Society of Comic Book Collectors? In Washington? I had no idea. Since it was past five, I thought I would have to continue this the next day. So, I turned once again to the 24/7 mighty computer. I typed in, Comic Book Collectors Society, and there they were—they have a page on Facebook. I have a profile so the link worked.

The society had a contact button at the top of their page, so I clicked on it and sent a message. They posted on their timeline that they also have a group so I clicked on that as well and joined. I took a couple pics, created a post and walked away feeling pretty good that I made progress considering I got up so late. Within minutes, there was a ding on my computer. It was a notification, and it was from the Society, a member commented on my post and so as they say, the rest is history!

Over the next few days of communications, commenting back and forth with members, an administrator chimed in who said he knew exactly who I was talking about and said he pinned my post to the featured section. This kept my post at the top of the group and soon after I found myself responding to a moderator who was also listed as an expert, Ms Marie Sovereign. She said she saw my pinned post and told me she felt goosebumps all over while looking at the pictures I posted.

A few minutes later, I received a private message via messenger. It was Ms Sovereign, who indicated it may be best at this time to keep a low profile. She confided in me that within the Society, there is a subcommittee—an elite group of scholarly individuals whose offices were downstairs from hers, some several floors below the society's office, literally, in the lower levels known as The L.O.O. or The League of Origins. A non-social media connected group of specialists whose mission is to document the origins and lives of superheroes, inclusive of all ages, especially those from the Golden Age, Including Miss Victory!

Ms. Sovereign seemed certain that the L.O.O. would most definitely have the information I was seeking and would be thrilled to receive an inquiry into what she described as the greatest age of them all, the Golden Age. She indicated that in her earlier days, during the end of the Silver and beginning of the Bronze Age, she was a librarian in the L.O.O. and did indeed hear of Miss Victory, but she had no specific information to share about her origin or whereabouts.

During our conversation, she mentioned that members of the league live their lives in the cool dry darkness, among the old paper they are sworn to protect, a low-profile quiet existence and informed me they can only be contacted through the old fashioned snail mail method, the United States Post Office. Marie explained, because unlike electronic communications, US MAIL leaves a paper trail.

She explained the procedure quite thoroughly, that letters of inquiry, which is what she said I needed to write, are scanned into the record by the secretary on receipt, and that the original is filed in the L.O.O. archives, a copy of which is sent to the clerk on duty for review. If the clerk feels your letter merits further attention, it shall be placed in the general mailbox to be copied and distributed to each member of the committee prior to their meeting on Tuesday. She informed me that the L.O.O. does not have a page or group similar to the C.B.C.S. but added some members of the comics society do intern at the L.O.O.. And the reason why she PM'd me. She wished not to compromise my submission mentioning I may have let the cat out of the bag by posting in the group. She explained that should the committee decide to share my inquiry with all its members, they will publish the letter on their private, members only website. Where it will be instantly accessible to the leagues entire community, domestic and abroad.

I was curious as to why the L.O.O did not have an above ground space and asked Marie if it was because the rent is lower underground, but Marie explained that was not the case at all — rather, the reason the L.O.O. is confined to the lower levels is because It's much easier and less expensive to control the temperature and humidity that is vital to the long-term storage of early, inexpensively mass produced acidic paper, namely pulp paper, which is what most Golden Age comic books are made of and printed on. During the 2nd World War, comics were not expected to last beyond the next paper drive and one of the reasons why many comics from that time are so coveted by collectors, especially those that survive in like new condition. As I was listening to Marie, I felt a great appreciation for the website I found where I saw and read the exploits of Miss V prior to, during and after the war, all at no cost.

Ms. Sovereign provided me with the address and suggested that I type, not write, for clarity, and sign my letter of inquiry, and mentioned it's probably best not to mention the suit at first, rather simply establish contact to get the ball rolling and hear what they have to say about Miss Victory. Needless to say, I did just as she suggested and composed a letter to the organization, inquiring as to what information the L.O.O. was willing to share regarding Miss Victory, such as where she came from and her current whereabouts, making sure not to mention the suit or the papers that emerged from it.

Chapter 2: A Gift from the Past

Several weeks later, seven to be exact, I received an old-fashioned snail mail reply from the League. Removing the letter from my mailbox and seeing the hand placed canceled out crooked stamp gave me the sensation that I was being communicated with by a real place with real people and not that of artificially generated intelligence.

Dear Stephen, Thank you for your interest in the history that took place during the golden age of comic books. The golden age of the comic book in America was and still is considered by comic historians to be the most significant age in the history and folklore of comic books. The golden age was not only the time when the superhero, as we know them still to this day, was born into existence, but it was also the time in history when America and the world needed superheroes the most. Not only did the superheroes battle evil head-on, but even more importantly, they inspired countless others to rise to the occasion and come together in an all-out team effort, stretching to all corners of the globe. Thankfully, they were successful in their efforts. Who knows if freedom would exist in the world today if not for the superheroes that emerged during the golden age.

Because our files are limited insofar as Miss Victory's origin and whereabouts are concerned, the committee has communicated with all of its members in all continents regarding your inquiry, requesting any and all information regarding Miss Victory, from her earliest appearance and origin up to her current status. We are saddened to inform you that in both cases, we can share with you only minimal information when it comes to Miss V, none of which informs us of her origin, and also there appears to be no verified information as to her exit from the superhero scene. Miss Victory's file remains the same as it has been since the L.O.O. was created. No updates have been filed since. Our listing for Miss Victory remains the same - Origin unknown, current status unknown - rubber stamped, MIA. Missing in action. File - Open see comments.

Members across our entire demographics appear to be very

excited yet reserved in their response since becoming aware of your inquiry, which is quite puzzling since Miss Victory's file has been dormant for years. Several members have indicated they were under the impression you had information to share that surfaced most recently. This seems to have caused a considerable amount of speculation that is circulating within the league as to the existence and disappearance of one Miss Joan Wayne, who we know from Helnit documents submitted to the general files after the war, was allegedly known to be Miss Victory.

Please be aware that it is the League of Origin's and its members' sworn duty to locate, collect, study, preserve, conserve, and correct information on the exploits of all superheroes, dating as far back as June 1938 up to present times. Some members choose to go back even further.

There is a great debate within the league as to when the golden age ended and when the silver age began, but that does not concern Miss Victory, as she is not known to exist in the superhero universe after 1946, which many members have come to call the Atomic Age, and well before the Silver Age began at the onset of the second half of the 20th century, just beyond the Initiation of the code of comics that formed in 1954.

It should be noted that there exists another woman superhero on record in modern times, that the league believes to have been inspired by and named after Miss Victory. Ms. Victory appears to be much younger and there is also a difference in the spelling of her name. We do not have her contact information at this time however we are 99.9% confident she is not one in the same as the Miss Victory in your inquiry and discussed here.

It has long been rumored that Miss Joan Wayne, aka Miss Victory, was captured by the Axis powers soon after the end of WWII and sent to Germany as a gift for Adolf Hitler, to be tortured, studied, and experimented on. There were also reports of Hitler's alleged demise in a bunker somewhere in Europe at about that time. Some members speculate that Miss Victory may have been at that location battling the Axis when the mountainside bunkers were bombed by the Allies. Many have assumed like so many others, Miss Victory may have been a victim of friendly fire therefore listed as missing in action.

There are other rumors that offer speculation that Miss Victory became pregnant during a mutually consented encounter with a black GI at the end of the war and that she has since gone into seclusion. This may hold water since there is a brief mention in the Captain Aero memoirs, which states: 'Miss V wants a family.' Several members suggest that this is pure propaganda from the Axis, created to distract from Miss Victory's capture, whereabouts, torture, and demise. This was known to be the Axis' method of operation, consisting of psychological warfare.

Verified sources at Continental Magazines document that the last known actions and whereabouts of Miss Victory is, that after a brief meeting with U.S. General Marlowe, an escort accompanied her to a nearby airport where she boarded her auto-seaplane and was spotted heading due east over the Atlantic Ocean, never to be seen or heard from again.

Otherwise, as it is written in her files, her origin and current whereabouts are unknown. In fact, her origin is completely nonexistent anywhere in comic book superhero history. To reiterate, all that is known of Miss Victory has been documented during the war by Frank Z. Termerson's Helnit Publications, Et-Es-Go and Continental Magazines. Sometime in 1944, the earliest missions were retold by Holyoke Publishing in an experimental one-shot format. All of these entities and their affiliates have long since become defunct. As originally reported by Charles Quinlin and Alberta Tews, and later by L.B. Cole & Nina Albright.

And let us not forget to mention the unknown, in this case unverified, among other contributors, Saul Rosen is suspected of reporting the very last known mission of Miss Victory in Captain Aero #26, published August 1946. There is still some debate over who is responsible regarding Miss Victory's last and final appearance. It should be understood that missions are not written, drawn and published until at least a month or more after the events occur.

A long-esteemed colleague of the LOO. Alex Kirby, a Golden Age specialist, wishes to inform you... and remind some of our colleagues, if they are not already aware.

In regard to the Golden Age, in addition to the known heroes who came to the world's defense during the Axis threat, there were many other unknown and undocumented heroes who took up the mantle of the superhero both on and off the battlefield whose stories and the documentation that supports their existence, have been either lost or destroyed due to the limitations in technology and the media that existed at that time.

Many technologies were not perfected, and the media used for documentation during those volatile war years were not stable and have deteriorated over time depending on the conditions in which they were stored, quite frankly, not made with longevity in mind. Most data formats that existed at that time were experimental, many utilized the cheapest materials, some designed to self-destruct after a specific amount of time once exposed to air. Microfiche used at that time was specifically designed for the war effort against the Axis powers of which employed extreme measures to prevent information from falling into the wrong hands.

We must be vigilant in our mission to preserve what we have left. As custodians of these artifacts, we have a responsibility to employ proper storage conditions including the use of acid free storage materials for our purpose and pledge as members to pass on our ephemera to future generations. Brittle documents cannot be made supple, but supple documents can become brittle, and this never ending deterioration has become our greatest foe. Once paper becomes brittle, there is little time left before it turns to dust. This is why storage conditions and materials used for rare and historical documents, particularly those made of pulp fiber, are of utmost importance without room for error. No compromise should be made. No expense should be spared.

In conclusion, as I believe all of our members are aware, there were thousands of men and women prior to, during, and after the war who carried out their missions in complete secrecy that did not live, did not survive long enough to tell their fate yet were victorious in their efforts. Sacrificing themselves for the future well being and safety of others, without reward or recognition. This was, still is and forever will be the cost of freedom.

The LOO would like to thank Alex for his insight. Indeed, it should be realized, understood, and remembered that many undocumented failures and successes have fallen into the realm of the unknown and unverified. However, we must never take the unknown and unverified efforts for granted or allow them to be forgotten. It is, in fact, the L.O.O.'s duty and mission to investigate, both individually and especially as a group, in an organized fashion to share and archive what we do know about those heroes and events as accurately as possible, even if there is little to no information available. There always exists the possibility that crucial information is yet to be discovered. Thus, all files must remain open.

The L.O.O. would like to take this opportunity to express gratitude toward Miss Victory and her many accomplishments. Because Miss Victory disappeared soon after the war, she may not be as well-remembered as she should be. She was not one of the more famous or powerful superheroes, but she was one of, if not the first, female patriotic superheroes to appear on the front lines before, during, and in this case, just after the end of the war. Miss Victory was highly intelligent, resourceful and extremely effective in her efforts. Perhaps even more significant was her influence as a leader in the concept of patriotism and loyalty to one's country, which is in itself a most powerful tool, especially when at war with such evil-minded foes, particularly those of the Nazi variety.

Miss Victory was unquestionably a genuine inspiration to those who followed in her footsteps, both female and male and those in between. She deserves to be kept in our fondest memories as a pioneer in the world of superheroes, for she broke the mold in a male dominated profession. Miss Victory appears to be the first real female of her kind.

That being said, we must also mention another female superhero, who carried the flag of the United States of America but disappeared just before the Axis powers engaged with the United States, known as U.S.A., the 'Spirit of Old Glory'. However, she did not appear to have a physical form. Due to this phenomenon, we must consider her a spirit, a ghost from a patriot's long past, perhaps even of supernatural nature, sent by God. There were reports in Quality Publications' FEATURE about her. For this reason, with an open mind, we must list Miss Victory as the very first patriotic superheroine in our records, in accordance with our current Overstreet guide.

Should you have any other questions or concerns regarding superhero patriots or any other superheroes, sidekicks, super vixens and villains during the previously mentioned ages, including the platinum, gold, silver, bronze, copper, diamond, current and future ages, please do not hesitate to write to this league's offices. We have enjoyed the discussion and awareness that your inquiry has brought to the attention of this league and its members. Regards, Max E. Newman, The Basement CBCS, attention the L.O.O. 101 Freedom Ave, Washington, DC. 10001

After hearing the league's response and the recognition given by the League of Origins' in appreciation for the significance of Ms. Victory and her impact on the United States of America and freedom-loving nations, I have come to the decision to donate the trunk and all its contents to the L.O.O.

Dear League of Origins, Please consider this trunk and all of its contents a gift to your esteemed organization. I believe this artifact rightfully belongs in your possession. Enclosed you will find a trunk dating from what appears to be from the 1950's. Inside the trunk, you will find what appears to be a hand made suit that I am certain you will find once belonging to the original Miss Victory, also known as Joan Wayne, as confirmed in the L.O.O.'s previous response to my initial inquiry, accompanied by a handwritten letter, allegedly composed by the owner of the trunk and all of its contents.

The suit appears to be, according to the letter, Miss Victory's very first outfit worn by Miss Victory in defense of her adopted homeland, the United States of America, and possibly other heroic patriotic minded efforts. I trust that the league will positively identify and verify the authenticity of this outfit and the holographic letter which fell from the suit's inside pocket during the initial inspection after discovery. Given the historical nature of this artifact and its significance to your organization, I believe this item in its entirety should be held, studied, preserved and displayed in the archive of the L.O.O..

Please note that I have included a second group of papers:

a translated into English copy for your convenience. I strongly believe that these papers, along with the artifacts so included, will prove convincing in furthering your investigations and should shed some light on Miss Victory's sudden disappearance after WWII. You will also hear Miss Victory share her secret origin. I suggest you sit down while you read the translation.

After careful study and consideration of the contents before you, it has become apparent to me that Miss Victory was aware of your organization and believe it was her intention that the League of Origins come into possession of these artifacts. I must warn you, to express the magnitude of what you are about to read, the letter of Miss Victory's own personal account, by her own hand, informs us who she was and how she came to be, and the reasons for her delay in sharing her story.

Please bear in mind, Miss Victory also explains at the onset that she has been diagnosed with dementia, a debilitating sickness that involves the degeneration of the mind for which to this day, is still without cure. Her origin is in my humble opinion not only truly inspirational but a most astonishing revelation, one that will not only reveal Miss Victory's surreal origin to the world but more importantly solidify her well deserved legacy.

I would like to express my sincere appreciation for your support and dedication to the memory of superheroes both known and unknown, documented and undocumented, from the past, present, and future. May God bless the United States of America, and all those who have done their part in upholding freedom.

Thank you once again for your commitment to preserving the legacy of the superheroes.

Part 2

Chapter 3: The Hidden Castle's Secrets

This is my origin. Miss Victory.

I have been informed by my doctor that my latest enemy's identity is known as Alzheimer's, a form of dementia. They used to call it getting old. She explained that my earliest memories will be far easier to remember than my more recent ones, which is a bit odd, isn't it? So, I will try to write this down as quickly as possible before my condition worsens. Please forgive me for any errors or omissions... and any confusion my illness may cause. I assure you, it's not intentional.

If you are in possession of this letter, then you must know about or have my very first suit as well. All of my suits are very sentimental. They each remind me of where I was and what I did in them. But the others are not as significant to me as this one. At first, I wanted my daughter to have it, but she said I should donate it to a museum. Imagine... (laughs) she's probably right. I thought I may one day send them the very last one. However, my daughter has already confiscated it for her own use. Not to mention, it is far more fashionable and much more comfortable because of the "V" stitched onto the chest, and of course, well, this is all I can say about that. I can tell you; she takes after her mother. Oh geez, maybe I shouldn't have said that.

What was I going to say? Oh yes, that's right. Well, I'm not quite sure where to start. Let's see, well, first I must tell you, like anyone who fights evil from within a costume, to experience any level of success, one must live in total secrecy. They must. Any other way would more likely than not spell death. Not to mention, you wouldn't get any sleep otherwise. In fact, my life was secret long before I chose to live my life in secrecy, and that may extend beyond my years, quite possibly long before I was even born. You see, I was part of an experiment born out of a test tube. Yes, it's true. Knowing what I know now, this is what I have come to believe. Today it wouldn't seem strange, but during the time I came to be, the thought alone was pure science fiction. The fact is, I have been, and still am, ashamed to admit why I disappeared so suddenly just after the war ended, that is, the 2nd World War.

First of all, I need to tell you, my name is not Joan Wayne. I not only longed to forget my past and who I am, who I was, but feared that should my story become known, I may put those I love most in grave danger. Not to mention, they would probably disown me if they ever found out... the truth.

Of course, now that my own time will soon come to an end... it does for everyone, you know, maybe one day that will change but for now, that's the way it is, so before it's too late, I want to tell you. I really need to tell everyone. I do. Let's see, oh yes, what I was going to say is... This is difficult for me, so please, please try to understand. In the end, I can only hope you can understand and that you will forgive me.

Okay, let me start this way... As a child, up until the day came when I learned otherwise, I experienced and knew only the good in my father. After all, I was a child once, we all were, you may still be, I know I still am at heart... I knew him as a good man, and so when I was young, I was quite fond of him. You could even say I was proud to be his daughter. It's very hard for me to admit, but it's true. Hmmm, I've certainly made a mess of this already haven't I?

When my father walked into a room, people stood up. They respected him. People did not sit until he sat, or he told them to. Right up until the time I was about to turn seventeen, I thought of my father as a great man. He was an award-winning author, a politician that was once loved by the people. He was very popular on the radio. Everyone tuned in when he spoke on air. I realize now, of course, that it was not love. He was a leader of men, and the men who followed him, followed without even the slightest hesitation. I can assure you, they jumped. Even when not in my father's presence, I was treated the very same as if he were standing next to me...

I didn't realize it at the time, but I had been born and raised in complete secrecy, hidden from the world. I never went anywhere. I was kept, kind of like a pet, but a prized example, similar to a thoroughbred racehorse.

I was raised on a very large, expansive mountainside estate, in a glorious castle built by a king. The best way to describe it would be to say it was nothing short of a fantasy land, very much like Walt Disney's castles in Florida and California, only with hills and cliffs, and enormous hidden caverns hidden by the enormous trees that surrounded them.

I was never bored. I was always kept busy, mostly with sport-like activities, building my strength and my endurance. And when I wasn't doing those types of things, I was also growing my brain, intellectually with regular studies... like science and mathematics, as well as art and music. These things kept me entertained but the emphasis was mostly on agility and strength. Which is what my father focused on most. I think it was his intention that I be born a male but sometimes you can't have everything. The fact I was a girl, perhaps he pushed harder. Of course, I loved my father, so I did everything he instructed me to do, and I tried very hard to excel without showing any fear, or lessened determination, which I learned only gained his favor. Daddy seemed very happy and very proud of me, that I was his daughter. But that's what I knew at that time. Everything seemed normal because it is what I have come to know as normal.

I was brought up not just by my parents, well, that's what I came to know them as, or those whom I assumed to be my parents, but world esteemed Nobel and Pulitzer Prize-winning scholars. I suppose I should be grateful that I exist at all. Nonetheless, my teachers were professors in all aspects of knowledge, including chemistry, mathematics, art, music, physics, literature, history, and even astrology. The stars were very important to my father, so they became most important to me. My father instilled in me that his goal was that I would one day win the gold. And so I thought, this must have been the reasoning behind my name and this motivated me to never give up.

Chess, the game of strategy, was also very important to my father, and I would play with my professors. Can you believe I once beat Albert Einstein at chess! My father didn't play, but he loved to have chess-themed get- togethers with his friends. My father would say to me jokingly, "If you are ever going to rule the world, my little Idola, then you must at least learn to communicate with the world. I want you to learn to speak Italiano, Englese, Espanol, Francais, Portuguese, Mandarin, Russian, and of course, Latin!" (laughs) I giggled and agreed, "Yes, father."

Father was a fanatical collector. He collected only the most valuable and rarest examples. Most of the things that surrounded me came not just from other collectors and museums but those discovered recently that shipped directly from the actual places where they were found. Many of which were once thought lost to the world, but he found them, or perhaps someone found them for him and he rewarded them in his own way. He was extremely demanding, and he had a very bad temper reacting to any level of failure. Men who made deliveries were sure not to slip and fall and break anything. Father would throw a fit if he found the smallest chip on the floor.

Many of the furnishings we had were not only original from when the house was built but gifts from other countries' diplomats, emperors, kings, and rulers from far-off lands. There were so many masterpieces in oils and golden artifacts that filled the walls of every room, originating from almost all places and times in world history. Even the hallways and bathrooms were overrun with world treasures. Like I said, my father was very fond of the things he collected.

His most favorite pieces were from space, including, as ridiculous as it may sound, an alien spaceship. It did not look anything like the spaceships we have come to know today through artist renditions, in fact when you first saw it, you would never think that's what it was. Not aerodynamic in the least. It was found buried in a tomb in Africa along with a golden ibis stick said to have once been used to rule ancient Egypt who at that time ruled over all civilization, previously lost for untold thousands of years until it surfaced and given as a gift to my father on his birthday. The most important pieces were kept in a massive vault far below ground, accessed only by a hidden elevator in the basement, a storage facility second only in size to the Vatican. The only entry was through a secret door in the study, one can only wonder how it was built.

He was completely infatuated with the rarest artifacts. He used to mumble while he napped that finding the Holy Grail or the Fountain of Youth would be the greatest gift he could give himself. (laughs) Imagine. Always for himself. I think he was really all he ever thought of. But what did I know? It was fun living in such a place with amazing and important objects.

This made learning seem a never boring enterprise, and it was a lot easier to understand and remember history and art when the actual artifacts you were learning about were at your fingertips. The love of history was something my father and I had in common. That is what he spoke about most... history and his place in it.

I did not attend outside schooling. I had what you could say was the ultimate in-home school education. In fact, I had never left the property for any reason until the day I left. We were isolated from the small village down the mountain, but I did have one friend who was my own age. Her name was Joan. The person whose name I later took for my own. She wasn't very strong, but she had a lot of spunk. And she loved to talk, which is why I loved her so much.

Every weekend, Joan would visit, and we would do all kinds of things. Since she had very limited physical ability, we used to have conversations about everything kids at that stage in one's life talk about. We played hide and seek in the garden's labyrinth, which was quite extensive. If you didn't know its secrets, you could be lost forever. We also made up our own games. Sometimes I would climb up a tree, and Joan would lie down on the grass below and order me where to maneuver about in the branches.

Sometimes the eurasian red squirrels would cackle at me. They make a cackling sound to warn outsiders not to trespass. We were never attacked more than a cackle. These squirrels are a bit different compared to the gray squirrels we have in the states. We had a lot of fun. Joan's parents worked for my father in the kitchen, making sausages on Saturdays and strudel on Sundays.

There were other boys and girls about the place, but they were servants and did not like to talk much. They were always tidying up, fixing curtains, lighting and extinguishing candles, wiping up dust that didn't exist, acting busy, while waiting for other orders. The other five days of the week when Joan wasn't around, I... as crazy as it sounds, I became friends with the objects and artifacts that filled the rooms and hallways. You were never alone, every bathroom had at least one bust of Caesar or other mythological God.

Yes, I talked to them. It was like there was a constant silent party going on in my head with all the works of art and worldly figures. Paintings by Monet, Picasso, Van Gogh, the busts of Plato, Da Vinci, Michelangelo, Raphael, and... anyone who was anybody was present, they were all there. I love classical music so I especially enjoyed fantasizing with the likes of Mozart and Beethoven. I found the musicians were the most pleasant, maybe because they were so handsome. I knew almost everything about them, and I could even hold a conversation in their native languages. The pianists seemed to have the most brains.

It's true, my imagination had developed well beyond most. This was actually part of my training since as long as I can remember, to hold a conversation with someone who is not there... talk about improvisation. The only time I didn't have to use my imagination was when I was with Joan.

I can't remember exactly when it was, but I think it was about that time when Einstein asked me if I played chess, which I did not and he asked if I would like to learn and of course I agreed. Before that he only made short conversation, hello how are you and goodbye. Every visit thereafter we played a game of chess. Early on the games were over quickly but as I got better, a single game could continue for weeks, which gave me time to consider my next move, until the day came when I finally beat him and we never played again. I think I was 13.

I remember once overhearing Einstein explain to my father that he was a scientist, not a magician, but he agreed to do his best to advance my maturity. How could you help but not laugh? I thought of him more as a comedian because he always made me laugh. So that always stuck in my head. His face would appear serious when he was trying to be funny and look funny when he was serious! I came to realize that this was the technique he used to increase my perception of reality. And so this is when I began to connect on a whole other level with the people and things that surrounded me. I came to know Albert more as a friend than as a teacher. I was just a kid eager to please. Perhaps this was the reason his visits lessened at that time.

Chapter 4: The Perfect Specimen

The doctors who checked on me were more like scientists than any doctor I have come to know later in life, they were more like inquisitive experimentalists, who gave me all types of vitamin boosters and enhancements. I think this may have provoked the situation I find myself in today. They either had success or failure. There were no in-betweens. Short term immunity is one thing, long term another.

I believe the reason I was never taught about medicine and the human body is because I might have been more inquisitive as to what they were giving me. I can only wonder now about the long-term effects of the medicines I was administered. I was given either a shot or a pill for pretty much everything I did including weekly injections, for reasons unknown to me. In fact I'm surprised I was fed real food and not a pill for meals.

I thought my mind and body were just fine at the time so didn't understand, nor did I question when I overheard them speak amongst themselves about brain enhancement through electric shock treatments administered along with specially formulated muscle-enhancing drugs, steroids as they came to be known, became part of the daily regimen. It seems quite clear to me now, that I was pretty much the equivalent of a lab rat, not a human being. At the time I thought my father wanted me to have all the advantages science and medicine had to offer, all the chances of success. For my success was his success, or was it his success that was also my success? I did not think much of the future, or the harm being done to my body. When I was young, as most kids do, I lived in the moment and considered myself lucky to have been loved so much. Ha!

Father always seemed to be coming and going. You found out when he was about to leave and when he was about to return when you heard and felt the rumble of engines and the footsteps of large groups of men approaching from nearly a mile down the mountain.

My mother always seemed to keep her distance whenever father was about to leave. Oh, I haven't even mentioned my mother yet, have I? I'm not really certain, but I'd like to believe she was my real mother, though I'm not sure in what capacity, if she was used to nurture me as an infant and later stayed on to give the impression I was the product of a natural birth and upbringing. Who would believe the child they came to know was born from a tube. I mentioned that already, didn't I? In fact I was never shown any photographs from when I was young, nor any other time in my life. Which is pretty odd now that I think about it. Anyways mom never went anywhere with my father rather she would disappear to her chamber whenever he was about to leave. I don't think my father wanted to take her with him either, so they both seemed mutually satisfied. In fact mother seemed relieved when he left.

This gave Mom plenty of time and the freedom to pray. Mom's specialty, when not praying, was dieting. She called it "fasting." It didn't make much sense to me at that time. I loved to eat. If I didn't eat, I felt like I would die. But now I understand. That's usually how it works in life. Some things just don't click until you have reached a certain point in your life. I wish I had gotten to know my mother better.

Mom made such a great effort to make sure that I didn't eat any of the most incredible candies and chocolates placed almost everywhere in the house. She said they were not put there for me, rather they were there for my father who was diabetic and had low sugar from time to time. Mother warned if I ate them, I would become a diabetic too. So she explained, it was a test of my will power. And I will be the first to admit, it was very tempting. But I refrained. My father explained it quite differently, that it was a good source of fast energy that is occasionally needed by the body. I realize now that my mother was telling me the truth and not making excuses like my father.

I can hear my mother right now reminding me, "The mind must always have victory over the body, so you must have a strong mind, not just a strong body. It is better that you have a strong mind and weak body than a weak mind and strong body. They both need cultivation." (laughs) I think my mother wished I was more like my friend Joan. Perhaps it was my mother who made my friendship with Joan possible.

I never realized by that time the reason why my mother seemed to have so much pity for me. She made me feel inferior, even though everyone else seemed to think I was superior. All the attention was always on me. We lived in that enormous mountainside monstrosity with what I thought was everything there was to have or needed to survive and be happy. Though, staying in that one place kept the rest of the world so much further away than it really was. But I didn't realize how big it really was at that time until much later in life. Seeing in books is one thing, going to a far off land is another.

As I grew into my teen years, I seemed to have developed this force around me, one of confidence and determination. I was very positive about my own abilities. I think what kept me from a completely domineering fantasy state was my mother. She was then what I would call today the only normal part of my life at that time. My mother and father seemed complete opposites. She was quite beautiful and my father. Well, I didn't think much of his attraction other than he was the one I needed to please more than my mother, yet I never saw very much intimacy on their part, but I never had that on my mind, so I wasn't aware of the signs, or aware of how parents act. The only other parents I knew were my friend Joans and I never got to know them. I was more of a tomboy. Now that I think of it, I don't think I saw any hugs and kisses or any other types of affection. Their relations weren't on my mind so much then as they are today.

When there were parties and elite guests roaming about looking at the fine art and artifacts, mostly on the weekends Joan and I were the only children at these types of events, but Joan was shy and didn't stick out, but she liked to watch me perform and was always there for me. She was my favorite audience. You see I was, along with my father, the center of attention until my father suggested that I retire to my room, which I couldn't wait for because on those Saturday nights, Joan was there with me and we had sleep-overs.

Once while changing into my pajamas, Joan took notice and asked if I was feeling well, she said I looked like I didn't eat. As far as physical status, I was developing into mostly all muscle, with negative 3% body fat. Not exactly healthy, but I assured her I felt just fine. I would tease her about my capabilities. That I was far more powerful than I might have shown her. I assured her my actions and reflexes were without the slightest hesitation and confided in her of my special treatment. We laughed when I explained how great it felt to take down men three times my size in one swoop. I explained that my father had plans for me to go for the gold in a future Olympics. I explained to her that running and boxing were popular sports throughout the world, especially in America, so they were extremely important to my father. Joan seemed to know this more than I thought she did. I loved to talk about these things with Joan, things that I couldn't talk about with anyone else. We would fall asleep fantasizing about the things we would do together once we were adults. The places we would go. The things we would see together.

I seemed to train as I slept. Dreaming of the time one teacher mentioned to another that I would learn more if I had only been beaten once in a while by those I trained with, but I never gave them a chance to lay a hand on me or take a full swing. I had learned not to give them any chance, or allow any leverage for them to strike back. Still, I was feeling great, not only powerful but empowered to a point where I felt no intimidation as I once did when I first started my training. It's amazing what you can do in your sleep. And now that my body had grown, I had much more of a snap in my step, with a certain lightness on my feet. And I can tell you, it did give me a bit of an attitude. So much so that I thought I could do almost anything. It seemed a step above mere confidence. What I came to realize as I grew wiser is not to show my confidence to anyone else, except of course my father. However, once confronted, in a hand to hand combat situation, It's wiser to act weak until the moment when you strike. The idea is to catch your opponent off guard. Afterall, I was just a girl.

The special drinks I was given throughout the day made it possible that I did not tire easily, nothing like those energy drinks they have today because whatever it was that I took helped my body recuperate at a far excelled rate. The status quo was to get a double day's workout in a single day. If I was feeling capable of more I took it to stage 3. That's 3 days. One time it was pushed to stage 4 and I passed out and woke up in my bed the next day. Did I mention I developed the ability to absorb high levels of energy on impact. I think this is where my mind helped the most, maybe through the electric shock treatments, insofar as my brain telling my body how not to react. Simultaneously calculating the force of impact and how best to shift, just inches one way or the other can make all the difference you know, by both lessening the impact and simply ignoring it, mentally speaking. As I grew to adult size, I seemed to develop very thick skin. Maybe the experimental concoctions were working, maybe they gave me an extra layer or two. Probably a combination of that and Einstein's calculus along with my fathers constant brainwashing were paying off. How this was to affect me later in life is something I wish not to talk about.

I never ever hesitated when my father gave instructions or failed to give the answer when he asked questions. By doing this I seemed normal, like I was doing what everyone else did, coming to attention and reacting on his order. Perhaps it was easier for me because he was my father, and I always did whatever he told me to do regardless. I made it a point to be the fastest in response. I wanted to prove to him that I could do everything he commanded and that I was the perfect daughter. I once heard him mumble to himself as he watched me while I was training. "I want perfection, I must have perfection, I must have a perfect specimen!" I wanted to be the very best specimen. I was indeed brainwashed, wasn't I? So every morning, with a fish-based breakfast, like a good girl, I took my vitamins. Vitamins with names like V-31, N-34, K-13, X-29. Sounds delightful doesn't it? (laughs)

When I hit maturity. I could do just as well, and in most cases, better than any man. I had developed skills that more than compensated for my smaller structure, in fact my size may have helped, insofar as gravity is concerned. I guess I had become my father's "perfect specimen!" He would call me throughout the day, and I would run from wherever I was like a gazelle when I received notice that he wanted to see me.

And he would squeeze my arms as if it were a drill, at least twice daily. "My little Idola, you are so special to me, my dear. I have big plans for you. One day, you shall see!" All I could think of was that he was planning to enter me into the Olympic Games in 1936, but he didn't, maybe it was because I was too young. He attended, I stayed home and trained. What were his plans, 1940?

I think I mentioned there were often parties attended by my father's higher society friends, oh yes, it was most humorous so I must tell you about it, he would call out my name in his own special way, "I-DO-LA!" Whenever he did this, I knew exactly what he wanted me to do. Perform on demand a pre planned choreographed display of excellence. I would, without hesitation, get to my starting point to establish eye contact with my father. Once made, on his nod, I would proceed to put my hands up into the air and perform a triple somersault through the crowd of guests who would need to move quickly out of the way while they were drinking wine and conversing on my way to the landing point adjacent to the seat of the Bosendorfer concert grand. At which point I would graciously sit down, take one deep breath, just one, there was no time for a second and perform "Flight of the Bumblebee" to perfection at a highly elevated speed! Within two minutes, it was all over, and the guests would shout with exuberance, and then the party resumed as it was. That's when I could freely breathe again.

I did end up getting really good at performing under pressure because of these playful acts. I practiced different routines many times a day, so I was always ready. And so, at these types of events, it became a regular thing. I actually looked forward to those moments and would be let down if it didn't happen.

I must say, everyone should learn to type, of course, in addition to having excellent penmanship. Typing was one of the most valuable skills I developed at a young age. There are times when it's best to write and there are times when it's best to type, each has a purpose. In fact I know there is a reason why I am writing this but can't think of it at this moment. As I got older and my fingers got bigger, I got better... and a lot faster. Typing seemed to come easy for me, perhaps because I practiced on that heavy-actioned grand piano for two hours a day. I have to admit, I found it very relaxing to go to the piano when my physical training ended. I guess you could say, it calmed my muscles so it was great therapy.

After practice, I would hit the books for about an hour or until it was time to eat dinner, after which I would head to the library where I would spend the rest of the day until retiring with a good book. Poe, Dickens, Hawthorne, there are so many, until it was time for bed.

Chapter 5: Unveiling Shadows

Everything seemed to be moving along quite well, and then one night, my life turned upside down. Or was it right side up? It was August 29, 1939. There had been some commotion regarding one of the guard dogs, Apollo, he escaped his kennel to chase after a rabbit when he apparently stumbled upon a dead body, buried in a shallow grave just beyond the target range in the most remote area of the estate, not very far from where Joan and I would hang out under our favorite tree. Wherever Apollo goes, his brother Zeus is certain to follow. They are very intelligent dogs trained to howl when something is foul. They must have known this person was dead or they probably would have licked him to death trying to revive the body. One of the men in black must have been there soon after to make the discovery.

That following Saturday, I expected to see Joan and wanted to mention this to her. She loved Apollo and Zeus and was great with all the dogs, but she didn't show up, and neither did her parents. This seemed odd to me. It hadn't happened for as long as I could remember, and the fact that strudels and sausage were so important to my father and his guests made it even stranger. So, I asked Emelie, one of the maid servants who takes care of the section of the house where I lived. She said Joan and her parents left unexpectedly in the middle of the night last Sunday and went back home. I said, "Home? But why did they not come today?" Emelie turned with a smile, "To their homeland, Poland!"

I was not only surprised but a bit angry. She left without saying a word about this. I got over it when I figured it wasn't her fault. Her parents probably didn't want to say anything to her because they knew she would tell me, which would cause me to ask my father and make it harder. So, I understood but was quite saddened by it. Joan was gone and I felt very alone.

Joan never mentioned she was from Poland. I thought her home was in the town at the bottom of the mountain, which I thought was where she was born. I never heard any mention of her being from Poland, though it makes a lot of sense why my father employed her father. Who better to make kielbasa than a chef from Poland?

I never visited her in the village down the mountain because my father said it was too risky, that I could be kidnapped and held for ransom, so it was not allowed. Yes, father did say on several occasions that I was one of his most valuable possessions and to never leave the specified boundaries for any reason. I accepted this fact knowing my father was a very important man and one way to hurt him would be to capture his only daughter.

That night, just after midnight, I went into my ninja mode and descended down to the kitchen for a glass of goat's milk. It was just then that I heard my father speaking hastily to a group of men in the study. I snooped close enough to hear what he was saying. "I told you to take away just the father, for interrogation. I didn't say to kill him and his family!" His man in black did not say a single word. Father then ordered that the man who didn't carry out his orders correctly be taken down the mountain and shot. And that the other man, or as he called him, the idiot who chose not to dig the hole deep enough, be taken away with the first man to suffer the same fate. The officer accepted the fate of his men without hesitation.

Wait! What man, what father is he talking about? What family? It can't be! It was at that moment that I realized the bodies that Apollo and Zeus dug up had to be those of my friend Joan and her parents. Did I really just hear what I thought I heard? Who else could they have been?

Needless to say, my head was spinning, and I felt sick all over. A wave of weakness came over me, and I managed to make it back up to my room without being noticed. When I got there, I realized I had forgotten the milk. Could it be true? Was my best friend dead? Was this really happening? I thought what kind of monster is my father? Was the man in my father's study really my father, or was he an imposter? How could he do such a thing? Why? Just earlier in the day, I loved my father with all my heart, and now, I hated him with all my heart and wanted him to die too!

I went to my room and stayed there. I think it was for the next two days. I shook and cried, trying not to, but I couldn't help it. I did not want to come out of my room for fear of seeing my father. I told Emelie to inform my mother that I felt sick and wanted to have my breakfast, lunch, and dinner in my room. It was the weekend, and there was nothing expected of me. This was the time when I usually spent my time with Joan, but now I was alone. I didn't tell Emelie what I overheard. I was hoping my mother would come to see me, but she never did. Did she even know what happened? If she did and knew I knew, maybe she understood how I felt but realized there was nothing she could do to change anything so didn't want to upset me any further.

While I remained in my room, my emotions were still in a state of shock, and I didn't want to leave and take a chance running into my father. If he wanted to speak to me, he would have to come to my room directly which he seldom did, at which time I would blame my sickness on something I ate. On day 2, it was sinking in and getting worse, Joan still had not shown up with her family. I lay in bed, thinking about my life, the past, things that now somehow seemed to make sense, at least more than they once did. Many questions came to me—questions about who I was, what my father's intentions were and what I was going to do knowing what I know now. I thought I knew my father better than anyone, but the fact is, I didn't know him at all.

Was I to remain my father's little Idola? I really didn't know how I could face him again. But if I didn't do as he said, maybe I too would be taken down the mountain and shot? Though at that point, I might not have minded, I would rather die than continue living with my father. But that finality didn't seem like the best decision. I must, in the very least try, try to avenge my best friend first. But how?

I wanted to escape, but where would I go? Where could I run to? How could I even get away? I didn't know what to do. The only person I felt I could trust to say anything to was my mother. Though I wasn't sure what she would have said, except maybe suggesting we pray. I thought of going to her, but I fell asleep.

I woke up abruptly the next morning, just before dawn, when I heard the rumble of a convoy approaching the mountain. Many men and machines were here to pick up my father. He left in haste without the usual goodbye, which worked out perfectly for me. Did he know that I knew about Joan? I was so relieved he left, and my headache subsided at that very thought.

All I had on my mind was Joan, so I ran to my mother at the far end of the castle to speak with her about what I had heard. But before I could say a word, my mother explained that Joan's father had learned of my father's intent to invade, destroy, and take over his homeland. He was caught sending a message to warn his family. Mother explained that the men were only supposed to take Joan's father away to be questioned, but apparently, Joan tried to stop them and was shoved away. She fell to the ground and hit her head on a rock, dying instantly. When her mother and father realized she was dead, they both broke out in a rage and attacked the men in black. They were both shot dead.

My mother said they couldn't have been taken down the mountain to be given a proper burial, because that would have disrupted the town's people. So my father decided to keep them here, and the people in the village would assume my father was keeping Joan's parents at the castle for his own use, sort of a reward for Joan's father's good work, all the while hiding any thought of what may have really happened, and the village people would be none the wiser. It's not like my father would have been questioned as to their whereabouts.

My mother said I should pray for my father. I wanted to kill him, not pray for him. I was confused about why she opted to pray for my father instead of thinking first to say a prayer for Joan and her mom and dad.

Mom said my pathetic father would not be back for quite some time. And while he was gone, there would be more people lurking about than ever, specifically, those dressed in black. Mother said I was to be aware at all times, warning me not to speak harshly towards my father because I might be heard. As much as it hurt to do so, I agreed to continue acting as my father's beloved Idola.

It's true, from that point on, they were constantly bringing documents to and from the castle. Whatever came in was brought into the office next to the study first until the documents were reviewed by the top brass, sorted, and eventually brought to one of the five underground storage bunkers on the grounds. As far as I know, there were five, I've been in at least three, I had no idea where the others lead to.

The men and women in black were almost everywhere you went, in the house and everywhere else on the property, some stationed far into the wooded areas. The grounds were flooded with men in black. I was not kept from walking into the wooded areas, but I was always followed and watched. They treated me respectfully at all times. The men would indicate to me that I was very beautiful and how great of a man my father was, and the women would say how they loved my father as if he were their father. As you can imagine, this was very difficult for me to stomach, and I wanted to throw up on everyone who said these things. I had fallen into an anorexic state; I just couldn't keep anything I consumed in my body. It all felt like poison. I needed to formulate a plan. What could I do to help those my father waged war against?

Now seemed like as good a time as any to use my mind as if I were behind enemy lines, what am I saying, I was. Physical strength was not going to solve this new problem. I did just as my mother suggested and made it a point not to talk ill of my father, even when I thought I was in private. My hatred was kept in my mind only, never expressing my true feelings with my lips, pen, or voice. These were self-thoughts only.

I kept a close eye, counting the number of boxes that came in and which bunker they went into. What were all these documents about? I had to find out. I had to act.

I could go anywhere I wanted on the property, and I never even tried once to leave, I wouldn't get that far anyway. No one ever questioned what I was doing when found looking through the files. After all, I was the direct descendant of the person whom they all seemed to work for and worship. I was showing an interest in my father's work.

I had become a spy in my own home. Eventually, I found out what I needed to know, and it was beyond belief. Apparently, my father had been planning this for years—to conquer the world! And to think I thought he was just being funny.

It was obvious that he had gone completely mad. In the more secret files marked "halt," I learned that he was essentially using Italy and Japan to his advantage. He regarded them both as idiots and fools, but at that time, he had no choice. He needed them, but what he did was convince them that they needed him. They must have been very weak-minded to have let my father lead them into war. They too must have been consumed by thoughts of superiority and world domination which obviously drove them to insanity.

Part 3

Chapter 6: Vanishing Currents

The files revealed so much, everything was laid out in plain ink. If Mussolini and the Emperor of Japan had only known the truth, my father would have planned to kill them both once he achieved his goals. Mussolini was to be fed at a feast and then drowned in wine. The emperor was to be poisoned by one of his close relatives turned traitor, whom my father promised a certain group of islands in the South Pacific. Can you believe it? Hawaii! This is why Hawaii was attacked by Japan when they entered the world conflict.

Armed with this information, I had to decide what to do. Sharing this knowledge would not have been only dangerous but futile. I did not want to make the same mistake as Joan's father. It was his mistake that may have actually saved my life. If I had not learned firsthand of his actions from my mother, the same fate may have awaited me. Sending a letter to someone warning of danger was not an option.

I tried to keep my composure and not go insane myself, focusing on staying busy and alert. I had become and was stronger, smarter, and far more aware of the situation that surrounded me. When my tyrant of a father finally noticed me upon his return on April 1st, 1941, over a year had passed or was it two. He smiled at me briefly before going about his business, which I now knew what his business was, he was more interested in his quest for world domination than in me. I of course smiled back.

When he saw me again later that day, he put on his fake fatherly face and opened his arms, calling me his "Idola." Oh, how I came to hate my own name. I was not an object in his museum, or was I just another idol? I hesitated just for a second as I started to run towards him, as he expected. I was saved from his clutches when a group of men dressed in black entered. He immediately turned away and went into the study. I followed cautiously to see what was going on.

As my father entered the room, the man quickly stood and made the Nazi salute, but wait, it wasn't a man—it was a highly decorated woman! My foolish father sat down, and all was quiet. He stared at the woman for nearly a minute before turning on a fan and directing it towards her. He examined her closely, asked her to turn slowly, and even had her let her hair down to create some kind of wild effect. The woman of course did as he asked before presenting him some documents she had obtained during her mission, emphasizing their importance.

Once the documents were in my father's hands, the woman proclaimed firmly, "PROPAGANDA, The AMERICANS!" My father nodded and commended the spy on her excellence, as well as her physical appearance. He thanked her for her loyalty, expressing his satisfaction with her performance and sent her off with the entourage she came with.

After everyone left, including my father and his aide, I went into the study, pretending to want to see him. There, on the Imperial dynasty table, I spotted the American propaganda left by the woman agent. I took the one on top and went back to my room to examine it.

It turned out to be a magazine full of color comics. I had seen comics before, but these were unlike any I had ever seen. The propaganda pamphlet depicted my father on the cover getting punched in the face by a Captain from America dressed in red, white, and blue, with a star on his chest, holding a shield that matched his clothing, it was quite marvelous.

Despite not knowing him personally, I couldn't help but find his actions endearing. Perhaps it was because I yearned to have the same courage, to stand up against my father and deliver a resounding blow. In that fleeting moment, I discovered a newfound affinity for the Americans. However, I knew all too well that entertaining such thoughts could lead to dire consequences. The very notion of liking the Americans was a dangerous admission that could cost me my life.

As I delved deeper into the story, a question nagged in my mind: How could the captain and his friend Bucky be aware of my father's plans all the way in America, especially when the country wasn't involved in the war at that time? Determined to find answers, I hurried downstairs and gathered the rest of the materials. As I voraciously consumed the tales, an indescribable transformation took place within me. It was as if a switch had been flipped, igniting a fire within my body and soul, something beyond anything I have ever felt. For the first time, I experienced a sense of connection and solidarity with the Americans, recognizing that, like me, they harbored a deep hatred for my father.

The following morning, as I returned the borrowed materials to their original location, I discovered a petite metal file box conveniently placed on an adjacent desk, bearing my name on its surface. With no one in sight, curiosity got the better of me, and I eagerly opened the box, extracting a substantial stack of papers. Intrigued, I retreated to the solace of my room to peruse their contents, only to uncover a startling revelation: these documents revealed the purpose that was intended for my life, and I found myself vehemently rejecting any involvement. Absolutely not! I refused to endorse my father's delusional ideas; I would rather die than comply. Could it be that this was the very essence of my existence?

There was no clear indication of the stage my father had reached in his pursuit of world domination, but it appeared that he was on the verge of involving me in his plans. I couldn't simply remain idle and await my fate. Was my sole purpose to be a pawn in his scheme?

I knew I had to take action, but the question remained: How? At times, I had contemplated taking my own life, especially when my father was absent. However, I always managed to convince myself that self-destruction was not the optimal solution. What purpose would it serve? It would render my life meaningless, nullifying all the training and preparation I had undergone.

I aspired to be a force for good, a valuable asset to humanity, rather than a burden. The idea crossed my mind—what if I could somehow attach a bomb to myself, one that I could activate with a hug as I embraced my pitiful father? But the question lingered: Where would I even acquire such a device? I could have probably manufactured one, I have the knowledge but simply assembling the parts required may be cause for alarm to those who were watching. Many hypothetical scenarios swirled in my thoughts. Among all the contemplation I had about ending my own life, this particular plan seemed worthwhile.

By sacrificing myself, I would have potentially saved countless lives. However, fear and uncertainty plagued me. The most rational choice before me was to find a way to escape that environment and seek refuge in America. Just the thought of joining in on the fight against my tyrannical and dictatorial father made me think more clearly and positively.

The very next morning, an idea sprang to life within me. Risky as it was, I knew I had to act swiftly. Time was of the essence. Faking my death seemed to be the optimal strategy, the only way to secure my escape. Naturally, for my plan to succeed, it was crucial that everyone believed my body was lost. Aware of the potential hindrance from my mother, I kept my intentions concealed, refraining from uttering a word.

To execute my impulsive scheme, I deliberately remained at the back of the training group that day. Dusk enveloped us as we approached the rope bridge on our route back to the fortress. Once all my companions had crossed the bridge and were ahead of me, I seized the moment and took a daring plunge into the turbulent rapids below. It was a now-or-never decision—a risk I had to embrace, prepared to face the consequences with unwavering resolve.

As I descended into the water, a shrieking noise escaped my lips, intended to draw the attention of those ahead of me, fostering the illusion of a slip and fall. Acquainted with the river's nuances from childhood swimming lessons, I possessed a precise understanding of where I needed to make contact. I navigated the waters with the knowledge of a spot, nestled between narrow rock formations, that boasted the necessary depth to shield me from striking my head on the rocky riverbed. Fortuity seemed to favor me on that fateful day. Reflecting upon the events now, I am inclined to believe that divine intervention manifested itself, as if God had dispatched his angels to protect me.

Aware of the likelihood that someone might spot me during their dash to investigate the commotion, I assumed a lifeless facade by floating face down. Holding my breath, I extended my arms, using my hands as a shield to safeguard my head from the encircling rocks. Carefully maneuvering my body around the obstacles, I proceeded downstream, sustained by my dwindling air supply. My objective was to convey the impression of a life extinguished. Just after the first bend, I surfaced, confirming my whereabouts, and promptly swam to a location where I could emerge from the frigid waters.

Having attained dry ground, I swiftly sought refuge within the encompassing trees, swiftly discovering a dirt path running alongside the river. Without hesitation, I altered my course, ascending the stream. Reasoning that anyone present that day and the subsequent search parties would likely concentrate their efforts downstream, I anticipated they would overlook the possibility of my escape upstream. After all, lifeless bodies do not typically travel against the current. An astute plan, wouldn't you agree?

As I make my way upstream, those searching for me downstream will be left empty-handed, their efforts seemingly in vain. With luck, the search will continue further downstream, towards the underground caverns and the pair of waterfalls that cascade into a purportedly bottomless lake. Recounted repeatedly during my earlier years as a deterrent from venturing into that region, it is unlikely that anyone would conceive the notion of searching upstream.

I'm glad I didn't inform my mother because it might have led my father to suspect her involvement in my escape attempt. She could have been thrown in where I intentionally fell, and I'm grateful that I learned to play chess.

A few thousand meters upstream, I stumbled upon a seemingly well-hidden cavern. I entered and found a spot to remove my clothing, allowing them to dry while I rested. I tried my best to stay awake, fearful that someone searching for me might discover me upon waking. If that were to happen, I would have to claim that I fell in, managed to escape the river, and was trying to find my way back home. Though I likely dozed off, I made a conscious effort to remain alert. Fortunately, I woke before dawn and resumed my cautious ascent up the mountain, keen on avoiding any encounters as anyone could potentially be searching for me.

As I pressed on with my journey, I couldn't help but contemplate the fate of those who may have faced extermination due to my sudden and unexpected demise. It was a price I had to bear in exchange for my freedom. My plan was to continue northwest through the Alps towards Switzerland. The distance wasn't extensive for me, and my prior training in this terrain was about to be put to the test. Adrenaline surged through my veins at the thought of being discovered, but once again, a stroke of luck or perhaps the prayers of my mother guided by God's watchful eye aided me. I stuck to the woods along the path, steering clear of any roads I encountered along the way.

Chapter 7: The Birth of Miss Victory

The following morning, I chanced upon a group of individuals engaged in a conversation about the change in weather. Recognizing the shift in language, I realized I had reached Switzerland. I emerged from hiding and approached these people, explaining that I had been held captive as a slave in a castle on the other side of the mountain and managed to escape by vanishing. I provided them with the name of my friend, Joan Wyspianski.

These individuals appeared deeply concerned and assumed a protective stance. They concealed me in a wagon filled with hay, transporting me to Swiss authorities. Shortly after, I found myself in the home of a Swiss citizen, where the authorities came to see me. I informed them of my desire to reach America and reunite with my family, who had left Poland just before the invasion. Without any hesitation, they embraced me, nourished me, and arranged for my journey on a train to Paris. Accompanied by a guide, I made contact with the French underground, and within hours, I found myself aboard a ship bound for England.

The presence of my father loomed over me as the sound of his aircraft filled the sky, accompanied by the reverberations of bombs dropping in London across the channel. It felt peculiar to be moving towards the sounds of destruction rather than away from them.

A group of women gathered together, offering their prayers, while silence enveloped everyone else. Evidently, these individuals had grown accustomed to such circumstances. Though everyone seemed aware of who was responsible, I couldn't help but wonder if my father had deduced my whereabouts and intentions, questioning whether it was me he sought to eliminate with his bombs.

Soon enough, I found myself in England without setting foot on land. I was directed onto a much larger ship docked beside the one I had arrived on. Given a loaf of bread and a cup of water, I was advised to be patient as I prepared to embark on my journey to America. The news filled me with excitement, and for the first time since parting ways with my friend Joan, a smile graced my face.

That night, I abruptly awoke to the sound of planes overhead as we sailed across the vast Atlantic. Instinctively, I sought cover, fearing the worst. However, a reassuring figure, who could have been my grandfather, gently grasped my arm and uttered, "Do not be afraid, those planes are friendly. They are the good guys." Glancing around, I noticed smiles of agreement and nodding heads in every direction. A voice rang out triumphantly, "The Americans!" and a cheer erupted among the crowd. The man leaned in and whispered, "We will be in America soon." Silence settled over us, and I soon drifted back to sleep.

As our ship entered the magnificent New York Harbor, I was roused from slumber by a young boy next to me. He was biting into a loaf of bread and excitedly pointing at the statue I had heard so much about during my train journey to Paris. Apparently my history books omitted this. But there it stood, a symbol of freedom—a woman holding a torch, a gift from France to America. It was an awe-inspiring sight to wake up to, one I shall never forget, the joyous atmosphere enveloping everyone around me was palpable.

The harbor teemed with an extraordinary vibrancy, a spectacle beyond anything I had ever witnessed before. It was almost magical. The air was filled with the distant melodies of music, echoing from every direction. Some of it was unlike anything I had heard before; I later discovered it was called Jazz—an exhilarating, liberating genre. I was about to embark on what had only existed in my books—the new world.

Once we arrived in New York City, we underwent quarantine, questioning, and were handed papers. We were instructed to keep these papers close and present them when asked, particularly for procuring food. These papers also served as identification, providing information about who I was and where I came from. It seemed to be the norm wherever we went, ensuring that others knew how to assist us. I had been assigned to a place called Brooklyn, where I received warm meals, clean clothing, a shower, and a safe place to sleep. The people I encountered along the way were remarkably kind, so I followed their guidance and instructions.

The food was different from what I was accustomed to—greasier but undeniably delicious. The sheer number of people surrounding me was overwhelming; individuals freely expressed themselves, unafraid to engage in conversation. In fact, I don't think I had ever interacted with people quite like them before that moment. This was a truly new and different world, and I found myself thoroughly captivated by it.

As I walked the bustling city streets, the crowd was dense, with people jostling each other in every direction. Occasionally, there were accidental collisions accompanied by a smile and an apology. These people's behavior diverged greatly from what I knew. For instance, one man leaned against a pole, casually smoking a tobacco stick. He flicked the ashes into the air and extinguished the glowing end with his foot, yet no one tackled him or made an arrest.

I distinctly recall passing a group of men observing the passersby. Their smiles were directed at me, and they tipped their hats, uttering greetings. One man even exclaimed, "Hello, doll!" and a couple of others whistled. Another woman explained to me the reason behind it, and I didn't mind.

Everyone appeared to be living in a state of happiness and harmony, as though part of one big, joyful family. Ah, yes! This was truly a land of dreams. No one raised their hands in exasperation, clicking their heels together. Instead, they waved their hands and called out names from afar, eagerly saying hello.
Such genuine friendliness towards fellow human beings was a novel experience for me.

As I strolled through the city streets, I noticed small structures resembling sheds on nearly every corner. These sheds housed racks upon racks of magazines and propaganda—similar to the kind my father's spy had brought to him. A young man stood outside one of the sheds, proclaiming, "Get your comics here! Only ten cents!" They were easily accessible, requiring only a small silver coin in exchange.

I really didn't even need to purchase the magazines; there were young people reading and sharing them with each other everywhere I went, it was only a matter of time before someone handed me one. Within these comics, I discovered stories featuring extraordinary individuals, predominantly men of great strength, intellect, and supernatural abilities. They battled the world's evils, including my father and his friends— Mussolini, Hirohito, and other deranged minds, often scientists who had gone astray. There were other topics, very funny pages, there was detective and mystery and science and so forth but I liked the ones with the Nazi's getting beaten up.

Gradually, I immersed myself in the lives of the superheroes and the prerequisites for becoming one. If that was the path I intended to follow, I realized that creating an alias or alternate identity would be my first step.

I had already adopted an alias, but I contemplated whether I needed an additional layer of secrecy. I pondered over what name I should choose for myself. It was essential to have a suit that would conceal my true identity and learn to act as two distinct individuals. Ultimately, I decided to change my last name, not my actual last name, but the one assigned to me on my papers when I arrived in America.

Responding to the name Joan came naturally to me; she had always been on my mind, my only true friend. So, I retained Joan as my first name, as it instinctively made me turn and look whenever I heard it.

Among the superheroes I read about, one stood out to me. He appeared more intelligent than the rest, and I admired his distinctive personality, he had style and a sense of purpose in life, not to mention the cave he worked out of below his estate, reminiscent of the one I had recently left, and as far as I could tell, he was single.

As an adult, my thoughts naturally turned to men more frequently than before I came to America. Perhaps it was because the men here were so different from those I had known before. Come to think of it, I couldn't recall a superhero I had read about who wasn't single. Many had girlfriends, but I couldn't find one who was married or in a committed relationship nor could I find a female superhero who was adorned in red, white and blue, the colors of my new flag. There were men but no women.

Regardless, thoughts of this one hero dressed in black, with a cape occupied my mind more often than I cared to admit. Nevertheless, given the turmoil engulfing the world, pursuing a romantic relationship was not a wise idea. It seemed more prudent to accept that I, too, could never be married. However, I allowed myself to indulge in fantasies of marriage and the dream of having my own family someday. I knew, of course, that it was purely a fantasy for the time being, and so, at that moment, I decided to take his name and become Miss Joan Wayne.

Changing my name was a simple process, many people during that time were altering their names to make them more readable and pronounceable. Filing the appropriate paperwork was all it took. I presented the document I had saved from when I first arrived in America. And thus, officially, I became Joan Wayne. Indeed, it was much easier for others to read, write, and pronounce than Joan

Wyspianski. I will never forget my dear friend's former last name, but it was time to move forward in order to fulfill my mission.

Once I made the change of name official, I set out to find employment—a job, a career! The prospect was exhilarating. I would be compensated for tasks that society expected of me—tasks that were both accepted and legal. It all seemed reasonable, even liberating.

In addition to my new name, I needed to devise a superhero alias befitting my role. Being a girl, which was not the norm in the comic books I had seen and read, I decided to use "Miss" as the first half of my new name since I wasn't aware of any other Misses at that time.

It seemed like the obvious choice and responding to "Miss" came naturally. But what should follow? It was in that moment that my mother's voice resurfaced in my mind, communicating a profound thought, what she had said to me so many times in the past—that the mind must achieve victory over the body. And so, it came to me at that moment: Miss Victory! My purpose was to triumph and bring down those who were in cahoots with my father, or any person or entity that threatened to dominate the world.

Thanks to my exceptional typing speed and language skills, I swiftly secured employment as a bilingual secretary at a well-respected law firm. My boss was deeply impressed by my efficiency, accuracy, and ability to communicate with anyone I encountered. As my worth became apparent, my rate of pay increased.

During the weeks I spent there, I learned a great deal. However, the job did not provide the leads I had hoped for in my pursuit of the bad guys. Nonetheless, it afforded me the time and compensation necessary to live on my own in secrecy while I crafted the superhero outfit befitting my mission—a suit that would, or so I believed, erase my past. I designed the suit as an homage to America's flag and the first American superhero I witnessed punching my father in the face.

Then, one Sunday morning, I stumbled upon the perfect career opportunity in the classifieds—a courtroom stenographer! This change in profession, although less financially rewarding, came with the fringe benefits I had been seeking. This new position granted me unlimited access to a variety of the files I needed to complete my missions. Computers had not been fully developed until after the war. How much time that would have saved.

Nevertheless, these resources provided leads related to criminal activities and background information on anyone who gave cause for investigation. Through the friends I've made in the system, I gained access to the most confidential insider type of information produced by government employees, including district attorneys and law enforcement officials. *In* a Federal position, I had access to the top-secret files held by the highest-ranking officials, including judges and politicians connected to various governmental departments on both state and federal levels.

Tax documents were also within my reach, and I utilized them solely to trace the flow of money. Whenever a high-ranking official received or made payments from dubious or illegitimate sources, it served as a red flag and a lead. My primary focus was on transactions that embodied an evil nature, hindering America's position as the leader of the free world. I had no interest in individuals or entities concealing funds from the government for legitimate purposes, such as buying a new home or car, as these actions ultimately contributed to the American economy. Instead, I directed my attention towards questionable transactions which in most cases were quite substantial.

Gradually, I developed an uncanny ability to detect the presence of malevolent forces, identifying inconsistencies within both the free market and the government through various transactions. Whenever irregularities hinted at corruption, red flags were raised, and I knew I was on the right track. This is where I wanted to dedicate my efforts, where I believed I could be a valuable asset to the United States of America, my father's most feared enemy, my new home.

Though I relished donning my suit and springing into action to defend America against evil powers that threatened democracy worldwide, I seldom found the need to assume my Miss Victory persona once I connected the dots on paper. However, nothing compared to the energy and thrill of wearing the suit and embodying American values and freedom.

Chapter 8: Reflections and Reunion

Towards the end of the war, the experimental concoctions administered earlier in life began to lose their efficacy. My body deteriorated as the effects wore off, and I came to accept that I no longer possessed the abilities I had possessed a mere 48 months before. Thankfully, this only affected my physical self, not my mind. Consequently, a time came when donning the Miss Victory suit was no longer possible. I suppose you could say that I carried out my missions from behind a desk.

There are moments when sentimentality washes over me, and I yearn for the feeling of putting on that suit and striking a blow against evil. After all, I am only human.

Months after I first graced the streets and war scenes worldwide as Miss Victory, I heard of a new heroine in town, a fellow government official. They called her Wonder Woman, a naturally strong, talented, and courageous young woman, described as an Amazonian beauty. I encountered her once in a secret military facility, but I did not disclose to her my true identity. However, I avidly followed her exploits through the countless stories I read. Truly, she lived up to her reputation. Undoubtedly, she will continue her superheroic endeavors for many years to come, far more visible to the world than I could ever hope to be. I am simply grateful to have been part of the battle between good and evil, standing firmly on the side of righteousness.

Just as my superheroine days were coming to an abrupt end, luck once again favored me. I was fortunate enough to meet and fall in love with a kind and affectionate veteran who had served as a medic on the front lines in the Marines.

We would have never met if Robert hadn't volunteered during his leave at the hospital where I received treatment after a close brush with death. We immediately connected, especially when he made me laugh by expressing his colorful opinions about my father. I found his humor both amusing and comforting. In fact, I didn't wait for him to propose; I asked him to marry me, and he joyfully accepted. Thus, I became Mrs. Robert Mar... Oops, I almost revealed it.

Oh, how I regret that I still cannot disclose my true identity, at least not my current one. Perhaps one day, it will be known. But for now, you know who I was long ago, in the beginning and I hope you can understand why I didn't share all of this sooner.

The one thing I cherished about Bobby was that he never probed into my past. He understood that if I wanted to share something, I would do so willingly. Well... I did mention it once, just before our 20th anniversary. I wondered aloud about my mother's fate in Liechtenstein, and to my surprise, Bobby arranged a surprise trip immediately after we boarded a bomber, which he called our "second honeymoon."

I had no idea where we were headed, but it didn't matter. I would go anywhere with my husband; he was my superhero! Bobby continued his service in the military and eventually became a top physician with the rank of Major General. We led a wonderful life, constantly traveling between top-secret military research facilities. I cannot disclose their locations; trust me, it's dangerous knowledge.

So, anyway... oh yes, upon reaching Zurich, I had to put on my sunglasses to hide my tears. Yet, I must admit, it was quite splendid. We stayed at a magnificent hotel with rooms reminiscent of my childhood bedroom when I lived with my mother. It evoked both bitter and sweet memories. It felt more like a reunion than a honeymoon, but it didn't matter. I was with Bobby, and we were free.

The next morning, we headed southeast towards the castle and made a few stops along the way to enjoy the sights. Each time I stepped out of the car, I discreetly put on my sunglasses, just to be cautious. I didn't want to take any unnecessary risks.

As we drew closer, a wave of goosebumps swept over my body, and my thoughts turned to my mother. She used to say that feeling goosebumps meant the Holy Spirit was present.

I had a strong desire to ask everyone I encountered about my mother, to see if they knew anything about her. However, I restrained myself and simply observed and wondered. If I had asked Bobby to investigate her whereabouts, it would have involved the CIA and other government agencies, and that was a risk I wasn't willing to take. He might have discovered everything about me, and I wanted to keep certain things hidden. Is that wrong of me? He despised my father so intensely, and I loved him for it. I'd like to believe he would have taken it as a joke and laughed it off. I suppose, at that point in my life, I still felt somewhat insecure about my past.

We eventually found the property, and as I gazed upon the remnants of the estate, which had been bombarded by the allies and reduced to rubble, I took a deep breath. It was a relief to see that nothing remained. I could only hope that my mother had escaped before it happened. So, I thought of her and said a prayer, hoping she had found peace wherever she may be.

Now, I look forward to the day when we will be reunited in heaven. I believe it's safe to say that while I will never have the chance to make my father suffer, he will surely face eternal damnation in hell. Bobby knows. I miss you, Muadda!

But on that day, I didn't have to utter a single word to Bobby. He could see it in my face and hear it in my heavy breathing. He knew that I had miraculously escaped the hell that he and so many others fought to save the world from—a war that claimed the lives of countless young individuals, all for the sake of a world free from such tyranny.

The price of freedom is incredibly high. I wish it weren't so, but that's the reality of life. When will we learn that there are better ways to coexist without ruling over others? As Captain Fearless once told me, evil will never cease to exist. Good cannot exist without the presence of evil. That's why superheroes and citizens around the world must rise to the occasion, understanding that evil is not the path to happiness. After all, everyone has the right to live a life of happiness.

My father undoubtedly deserved every profanity Bobby and others hurled at him, and then some. Just the notion of attempting to eradicate an entire race as if they had no right to exist is unimaginable and unforgivable. I now realize that praying for my father might not have been such a bad idea.

I am immensely grateful that I never succumbed to the thought of taking my own life. Just the mere contemplation weakens me. Please forgive me for being saddened by the fact that discussing my father is necessary to convey my past. My family knows nothing about him beyond what they have read and seen on TV, and unfortunately, it's all true, and likely much worse.

What I truly want to emphasize is that just because my father was evil, it does not mean that I am evil, nor are my children. You see, evil does not always perpetuate evil. I can only hope that my documented actions have proven this to you.

With love always,

Idola von Hitler

Acknowledgments:

I would like to express my heartfelt gratitude to Charles Quinlan and Alberta Tews, the brilliant artist and author creators of Miss Victory and their collaborators who brought forth the concept of Miss Victory at a crucial time when the world needed a female character to challenge the boundaries of women's rights within the predominantly male-dominated realm of the patriotic minded superheroes.

Coming Soon:

A series of stories that delves into the events preceding Idola's experimental birth, from the very idea of her existence through her childhood and development, chronicling the circumstances that shaped her design & purpose and even the possibility of other individuals sharing the name Idola.